Just Breathe Evie!

W. Keith Wise

Archway Publishing books may be ordered through booksellers or by contacting:

Archway Publishing
1663 Liberty Drive
Bloomington, IN 47403
www.archwaypublishing.com
844-669-3957

Because of the dynamic nature of the Internet, any web addresses or links contained in this book may have changed since publication and may no longer be valid. The views expressed in this work are solely those of the author and do not necessarily reflect the views of the publisher, and the publisher hereby disclaims any responsibility for them.

ISBN: 978-1-6657-5593-1 (sc)
978-1-6657-5594-8 (hc)
978-1-6657-5595-5 (e)

Library of Congress Control Number: 2024901972

Print information available on the last page.

Archway Publishing rev. date: 02/01/2024

To Evie:

You're such an Evie.

Many thanks to my editors who keep me on track and focused: Sue Abernethy Davis and Kim Morgan.

Of course, My Best Girl Shirley Wise, Evie's Nami, is always ready to help me when I'm just missing it.

Just Breathe Evie

I once asked Evie,

do you know how much I love you?

I wasn't really sure she knew.

"Of course I know Papa," she said.

"Of course I do."

I said, "I'm not sure there are enough words Evie.

I love you more than I can say."

"Oh Papa, you needn't worry," Evie said,

"I know you love me every day."

But Evie, I don't see you every day.

How are you so sure?

"I always feel your love Papa.

More, and more and more."

How about when I pick you up from school?

Do you know it even then?

"I know it when I see you waiting,

I know it even then."

At your soccer games

Do you hear us yell?

"I hear you cheer, I really do.

Do you know I love you too?"

Do you know it when we go to the zoo

Or even to the movie?

"I always know it Papa,

I always know it's true."

What about making cookies with Nami?

Even when you're mixing dough?

"Making cookies is fun for us," said Evie,

"Even then I always know."

Sitting in your driveway or

swimming in your pool?

Do you know I'm going to love you

even when you're at school?

"I know you love me Papa,

I see it with ease,

I know you love me," Evie smiled,

"all I have to do is breathe."

17

Printed in the United States
by Baker & Taylor Publisher Services